For Alison and Nick

First American edition published in 1991 by G. P. Putnam's Sons, a division of
The Putnam & Grosset Book Group, 200 Madison Avenue, New York, NY 10016.
Originally published in 1990 by Orchard Books, London.
Published simultaneously in Canada. Printed in Belgium.

Library of Congress Cataloging-in-Publication Data
Anholt, Catherine.   Good days bad days / Catherine Anholt.—1st American ed.   p.   cm.
"Originally published in 1990 by Orchard Books, London"—T. p. verso.
Summary: Depicts many kinds of days in a family, such as school
days, sick days, snowy days, dull days, and fun days.
[1. Days—Fiction. 2. Family life—Fiction.]   I. Title.
PZ7.A5863Go 1991 [E]—dc20 90-38901 CIP AC
ISBN 0-399-22283-9

1   3   5   7   9   10   8   6   4   2

First American edition

Good Days Bad Days

Catherine Anholt

G. P. Putnam's Sons • New York

In our
family

we have

good days

bad days

happy days

sad days

work days

play days

home days

away days

sunny days

snowy days

rainy days

blowy days

healthy days

sick days

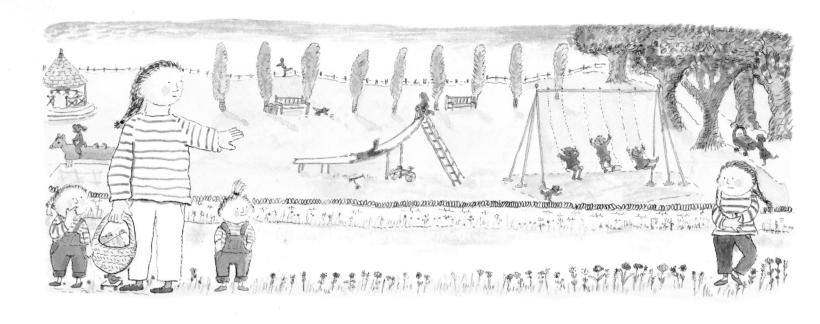

slow days

quick days

school days

Sundays

dull days

fun days .

Every day's a different day,

but the best day follows yesterday.

Today!